A SUDDEN STORM

BALI RAI

Illustrated by
David Shephard

Barrington  Stoke

Published by Barrington Stoke
An imprint of HarperCollins*Publishers*
Westerhill Road, Bishopbriggs, Glasgow, G64 2QT

www.barringtonstoke.co.uk

HarperCollins*Publishers*
Macken House, 39/40 Mayor Street Upper,
Dublin 1, DO1 C9W8, Ireland

First published in 2023

ISBN 978-1-80090-253-4

10 9 8 7 6 5 4 3 2

Printed in India by Replika Press Pvt. Ltd.

In memory of Ricky Reel, and for Sukhdev Reel and her family. Still fighting for justice so many years later.

And for all those human beings murdered and hurt in the UK simply because they looked different.

BEFORE

What if you lit a candle for each of your dreams? You stand them in a line, and the flames flicker and crackle. Even when it's cold, or you're not feeling great, you know the candles are there. That keeps you going. The flames light the way in every battle you face, for every problem that knocks you back.

You can't even see the candles, but you know they are there, in your head. And that's all that matters. You know they are there ...

And then a sudden storm. A howling gust of wind. The flames snuff out. Just blown out as though they never mattered. As though you never mattered.

In an instant. Nothing left ...

CHAPTER 1

My house that night was warm and light. It felt safe.

When I got in from school, Dad was in the new kitchen, finishing off the shelves. He was tall with strong hands and a big beard. His clothes were old and dusty, and his brown work boots had holes in them. He looked hot and cross as he tried to get the shelves level.

"Need a hand, Dad?" I asked as I shut the front door behind me.

"No, no," he said. "Go on up and get changed out of your wet clothes, Arjan," he told me. "You're soaking wet! Get ready to go out with your friends."

"I don't have to go out," I said. "It's not some major thing. We're just going to watch a film and grab a Nando's after."

"It's your sixteenth birthday, son," said Dad. "Go and have fun."

I grinned. "What were you doing when you were sixteen?" I asked him.

"I was farming in Punjab," he told me. "And two years later I married your mother. We didn't have bloody cinema and Nando's!"

He grinned too. "My life was different, boy," he added. "I don't want the same for you."

My parents were Punjabis – they grew up in the north of India. They were Sikhs, and I was Sikh too. That was our religion, and our way of life. Even in England, where I was born.

"I would be proud to be like you," I told Dad.

"Bloody hell!" he groaned as he dropped the spirit level. "Grab that for me, son."

I picked the level up and handed it to him. He looked at me for a moment. Then he hugged me.

"Time moves on, " he said to me. "We are British now, and you have more opportunities than me. I don't want you to waste them. Life is about moving forward. It is about doing well and being happy."

"I know, I know," I joked. "You want your son to be a lawyer or a doctor. Typical Asian parent ..."

Dad laughed. "You daft *bandar*," he said. "I don't care what job you do. Just do your best and be happy. Then I will be happy."

"I can be all of that and *still* help you," I told him.

Dad was a builder and worked long days, sometimes seven days a week. He loved his work, but he wanted more for me.

"I use my hands," he replied. "It's good, hard work. You are clever, boy. You can use your brain. Dream bigger."

"So builders don't use their brains?" I joked.

"Of course we do," he told me. "But you must follow your own path. Now, get going. You'll be late. It's your birthday."

"Are we still having a family party too?" I asked.

"On Sunday," he replied. "At the gurdwara."

Each year of my life, my parents held a service at our local Sikh temple. It was a chance to get our huge family together. To give thanks for our blessings. There was a big party after.

"Cool," I said. "Better get ready for tonight then."

He scratched his head under his grey turban. "Bloody shelves," he said as I went up to my bedroom.

CHAPTER 2

I wore a turban too. In fact, at school that day, I'd finished an essay about it. My school had an enrichment week every June, and this was my last chance to take part. I was leaving after my exams in the summer. The school librarian, Miss Khan, was keen for me to give a talk to the Year 7s and 8s.

"Go home, Arjan," Miss Khan told me after school. "You've been more than helpful today."

"In a minute, Miss," I replied. "Looking for a weekend book."

"How is your essay coming along?"

"Done," I told her.

"Are you still happy to read it aloud?"

I nodded. "Course," I said. "I know I'm leaving this year, after my exams. But I'll come back in afterwards."

"I'm glad you're happy to speak about your faith," she replied. "It's important for the younger pupils. You should get going though. It's Friday, and I need to lock up."

"One more minute," I said as I grabbed a book to borrow.

"And happy birthday!" she added. "Got anything planned?"

"Just the cinema and food," I replied.

I walked home down the high street. It was raining, and I could feel my turban getting really wet. There was loads of traffic. I heard car horns and swearing, and kids shouting and laughing. The normal sounds of my walk home. A gang of lads took cover just inside a fried-chicken shop.

"Yo!" yelled Yusuf, one of my best friends. He was thin, all long legs and big feet, and a goatee beard that made him look like a wise man from a kung-fu film.

"Easy, bro!"

"Come out of the rain, innit."

I shook my head. "Nah, I gotta get back," I told him. "Wanna chill at home."

"We still going cinema later?" asked Yusuf.

"Yeah, if you still want to."

Yusuf was always out and about. Even in the rain, after school. A proper roadman, people called him. But he wasn't into gangs or nothing. Not like some of the lads we knew. He was a joker and a good laugh.

"Course, bro!" he replied, stroking his little beard. "What time?"

"Film starts about seven, I think," I said. "I'll check and message you."

"Who else is coming?" Yusuf asked me.

"Tyler and Pavel," I said. "Maybe Kasia and Jem too."

"OK," he said. "Should be a laugh."

I left Yusuf and went on walking. The rain was heavy now and running down the back of my coat. My school shoes were soaked.

"Bring a waterproof turban though, bruv!" Yusuf shouted from the doorway.

I swore at him but laughed too. I didn't think or look but stepped out to cross the high street. Suddenly, I heard brakes squealing. A van stopped right by me. I froze in panic.

"You stupid prick!"

The van was white, like my dad's, and the driver and his friend were tradesmen too. The driver glared at me. The guy next to him was younger than him, with a blond ponytail and tattoos up his neck. He was grinning at me as if something was really funny.

The driver got out. "You thick, pal?" he yelled right up close to my face.

"Sorry," I replied. "I wasn't watching where I was going and—"

"Too right," said the driver. "You must have a death wish."

"Probably can't hear with that nappy on your head," said the guy with the ponytail from his window. "What are you – Taliban?"

I felt my stomach turn. My legs shook a little. "I'm a Sikh," I said. "Sorry again. Didn't mean to upset you."

The driver shook his head. "I can't stand you immigrants," he told me.

"I was born here," I said. Even though I was still scared.

"Don't mean nothing to me," said the driver. "You ain't English with that stupid rag on your head!"

"It's called a turban," I told him.

"Call it what yer like, pal," he replied. "Now, piss off back to India, mate."

As he jumped back in his van, the young guy grinned again. "Go home and build a bomb," he said.

He spat at me, and then they drove away. I didn't move for a minute. I wanted to stop shaking first. I was angry and scared at the same time. I wanted to chase after them and tell them what a turban was, and who I was. And I wanted to punch them too. But I told myself to cool down and remembered that I was a Sikh. I would defend myself if I needed to, but I wouldn't start a fight.

"You OK, bruv?" I heard Yusuf asking behind me.

"Yeah," I said. "Just a couple of idiots."

"Sorry, I should have seen it sooner," said Yusuf. "Them man need a proper kicking."

"I feel sorry for them," I replied. "They're just ignorant and angry. Nothing to worry about now, anyway."

We bumped fists, and I went home.

CHAPTER 3

Back home, after I'd chatted with Dad, I went up to my bedroom to get changed out of my wet clothes.

I stood in front of my mirror. I liked to look at the way it reflected my Arsenal FC posters, my bed, and three shelves loaded with books and old toys and other stuff. Then I began to take off my wet turban. Like Yusuf said, it was soaking.

My school turbans were black, to match my uniform. I also had other colours, which I wore outside school. I'd worn a turban since Year 7. Before that, I used to have a topknot covered with a tied white handkerchief.

I had never cut my hair, so it was thick and long. I washed it and oiled it to keep it healthy. But I'd never cut it. My friends often asked if long hair was annoying or difficult, and sometimes it was. But it was also part of who I was.

I wanted to shower and get dressed in my casual gear, so I unwound my turban slowly and put it on my bed.

The racist men from earlier bothered me. They were small-minded and ignorant. What did they know about turbans? Mine was like my Sikh crown. It showed the world that I was a *Singh* – a name that all true Sikh men have. Sikh women are known as *Kaur*. Sharing these names shows unity, that all people are one. Sikhs don't believe in prejudice. It upset me that those men didn't understand that.

See, most people didn't get my turban. Not really. I'd had abuse a few times, but mostly just ignorance and rubbish. Even my mates made jokes, although I didn't mind that because they meant no harm. It was just banter, and we all did it.

We never joked about the serious part though. My friends knew that wearing a turban was about self-respect and courage. It was about showing that I loved my friends and my family more than myself and I would put myself second. My friends respected that, and they respected me. I wasn't going to let those racists get to me. I was a British Sikh, and their ignorance was their problem.

After my shower, I dressed in black jeans, a matching T-shirt and hoodie, and my white Adidas trainers. As I sat to retie a different turban, Mum knocked at my door.

"Come in."

As soon as she entered, she took the fabric from me. "This is for school," she said. "Wear one of your other turbans."

"But this one matches my clothes," I told her.

"Don't be silly," she told me. "It's your birthday. A splash of colour won't hurt."

Mum opened my cupboard and took out some red cloth. Arsenal FC red, or so I told people. "This one?" she asked.

I nodded. "Go on then," I said. "Just for you, Mum."

"You will look wonderful!" she told me.
"A true Singh!"

She wrapped the cloth around my head
before fixing it. Once she was done, she
smiled. "Perfect," she said.

"Thanks, Mum," I replied.

"Your friend is here," she added.

"Huh?"

"Tyler," she told me. "He arrived when you were in the shower."

"Why didn't you tell me?"

Mum grinned at me. "Why does it matter?" she asked. "He's downstairs eating samosas."

I laughed. Like me, Tyler loved samosas. It was probably the only reason he'd turned up. He was waiting for me in the living room, watching one of Mum's Indian channels on Sky. An old Bollywood film was playing. Tyler had reddish brown hair styled in cornrows, and wore a big orange puffer jacket.

"These films are mad, bro," he said. "Someone just got shot, and now they're dancing around the drummers!"

"They get worse," I told him. "You should see the drama shows too. They're proper whacked out."

"Nice threads, bro," Tyler added. "That turban is sharp!"

"Mum made me wear this," I said. "I was gonna wear a black one."

"Nah," he replied. "It's your birthday, bredda. Gotta show up in fine style, innit. Might even impress Jem ..."

"Doubt that," I replied.

I'd never had a girlfriend and wasn't exactly looking. But Jem was nice, and she seemed to like me.

Things were changing. I had GCSEs coming up, and then I was leaving school to do A Levels at college. My world felt wide and open and full of opportunities. Adult life was coming soon, and I was excited. As much as Tyler was excited by my mum's food.

An empty plate sat on his lap, with a blob of ketchup on the side.

"You enjoy the samosas?"

"Yeah," he said. "Delicious, as always. Was gonna save you one, but you know how it goes ..."

As he licked his fingers, Mum walked in with another plate of samosas and two cans of cola. "Eat up," she said. "It's cold and wet outside, so warm your bellies."

"Guess it would be rude to say no," said Tyler.

"Like you'd say no anyway," I told him. "You don't *ever* refuse samosas, bro."

"Yeah," he said, his mouth full. "Cos I ain't dumb, you get me?"

"Have a good night and be careful," said Mum when we were done eating.

"I will," I promised. "Back by 1 a.m. latest."

Mum smiled. "Make it midnight," she said.

"OK," I told her.

I checked my turban once more, grabbed my coat and left with Tyler, who had put another samosa in his pocket.

"I should charge you for them," I joked.

"Nah!" he mocked. "I thought you Sikhs was all about sharing and family, bro. Only reason I've been your mate since Reception, innit!"

"Shut up, you moron!"

CHAPTER 4

We met Jem and Kasia by McDonald's and then caught a bus on the high street. The cinema was about twenty minutes away, in another part of the city.

We were cracking jokes and having a good laugh, and I was happy that Jem had made it. We'd been good friends since Year 7, and now there was something else happening. It was exciting, but I was nervous too.

We met the others at an "Entertainment Village", which had a bowling alley, restaurants, dessert parlours and stuff. Behind was a huge retail park and the riverside.

"What we watching again?" asked Pavel.

He was the tallest of us, with blond hair and pale blue eyes. He spoke with a bit of a Slovakian accent, but he'd lived in England since he was seven. He'd been my friend all through primary school.

"Action-type thing," said Yusuf. "But I only got four tickets."

"It's OK," said Kasia. "We can get our own."

"I'll get them," I told her. "It's my birthday."

Kasia was half Polish and half Welsh, with jet-black hair and bright green eyes. She reminded me of a cat.

"Yeah," said Jem. "That's exactly why you shouldn't pay for us!"

"It's a Sikh thing," I replied. "Like, nothing sexist or anything. Just a thing I got from my dad."

Jem and Kasia looked at each other. "OK," said Jem, "but we're buying your snacks. Deal?"

"Deal," I said.

"So, what are we watching?" asked Kasia.

"Some action film, like I told you, innit," replied Yusuf.

"You booked the tickets," Pavel said. "Why can't you remember what the film is?"

"Who cares?" said Tyler. "Let's just get inside before the rain gets heavy again."

We messed about for ages, getting popcorn and slushies and sweets. By the time we got into the screen, the trailers were on and it was dark.

Luckily, the rain had kept people away and it wasn't busy. Good job too, because we were a bit noisy. Nothing mean or nasty though. We were just having fun.

Some people did that coughing thing, to show they wanted us to stop joking around, but no one spoke up. I started feeling bad for them, so I told my friends to calm down.

The film was good, and afterwards we walked through the rain to Nando's. There was a small queue, so we stood and waited. The front of the building gave a bit of shelter. But we were soaked anyway.

"I'm drenched," said Jem.

She was as tall as me, with curly dark hair and a wide and ready smile. Her mum was a nurse, just like mine, and they worked together.

Jem's dark eyes reflected the street lights as she moved closer and gave me a hug. Her perfume was spicy and warm smelling. Then she shook her hair and droplets of rainwater flew off.

"Gerroff!" I yelled, wiping my face.

"See?" she said. "Told you!"

We messed about a while longer before being let in. I was desperate for the toilet, so I asked Tyler to order for me.

"No worries, bro," he said. "Ten per cent interest though."

Jem gave her order to Kasia and came with me. "You having fun?" she asked.

"Yeah," I told her. "It's great that you could all come out."

"You mean me mostly though, yeah?" she joked.

I shook my head. "Nah!" I teased.

Jem punched me on the arm. "Don't get cheeky," she warned.

"Well, yeah," I said, getting a bit embarrassed. "I like you."

Jem grinned. "Obviously," she replied. "And why wouldn't you?"

Someone shoved past me, but I ignored it. The restaurant was packed, and the tables were close to each other. It was tight.

"See you back at the table," said Jem. "Love the red turban by the way. You look cool. Like a prince."

I smiled. "Thanks," I replied.

The gents was empty, apart from someone in the cubicle. I could hear them sniffing, and then they coughed a bit. I finished up and began to wash my hands. The cubicle toilet was flushed, and someone stepped out.

"What we got here then?"

When I looked up into the mirror, my stomach flipped. It was the lad from the white van. Mr Ponytail.

"You following me, Taliban?" he added with a nasty grin.

He wore the same clothes as before, and I could see his safety boots now – big and black, with steel toecaps.

"I'm just having some food," I replied. "I don't know you, and I don't want any trouble."

"I ain't giving you any trouble," he replied. "But you were chatting up a white girl, and that ain't right."

It must have been him who'd shoved me in the restaurant just now.

"She's a friend," I said. "And it's none of your business."

He grinned again. "Dirty little raghead," he said, and walked out.

Back at the table, I didn't say anything. We were having a laugh, and when I saw Mr Ponytail and his two friends leave, I felt better.

"So, what now?" asked Yusuf when we'd finished eating.

"Walk back?" suggested Jem. "We could take the path by the river. It's stopped raining too."

I wanted to say no, but the others were up for it. I had a thing about open water. I didn't swim, and I never went into the sea on holiday. Open water made me stress, and I couldn't even tell you why. It just did.

"I dunno," I said. "It's late and ..."

"I have to get the bus," said Kasia. "Got a dumb curfew."

Tyler, who knew I didn't like water, nodded. "Don't worry, bro," he said. "We won't kidnap you or nothing."

As everyone else laughed, he whispered to me. "Relax, bro," he told me. "I'll walk between you and the river."

"Thanks, Ty," I replied.

"Besides, Jem *wants* you to walk," he quickly added.

"We could cuff him to a lamppost in his boxers," suggested Yusuf. "Like them man on stag nights ..."

"Does he even wear boxers?" said Pavel. "I think he goes commando, innit!"

Even I burst out laughing at that one. And in the end, I was more excited about walking back with Jem than stressed about the river.

CHAPTER 5

Kasia and Pavel took the bus back, and the rest of us walked. The path by the river was well lit and wide. Tyler walked between me and the water, so I was relaxed. Especially when Jem linked arms with me and started teasing Yusuf.

"King Roadman Supreme," she said to him.

"And proud of it," Yusuf replied. "You, man, are just jealous."

"I'm not a man," Jem pointed out.

"You know what I mean," said Yusuf.

"Street smart, innit. Everyone knows ..."

"Rats are street smart too," said Tyler.

"Nah, bro!" Yusuf replied. "How you gonna side with a girl and do me that way?"

Up ahead, I saw three men sitting on a bench, drinking cans of lager. My heart pounded. It was Mr Ponytail and his mates. If they saw me, we'd be in trouble.

"Let's move back to the main road," I said softly.

"Nah, this is fun," said Yusuf. "The river looks awesome."

"Be quicker though," I added.

Too late. Mr Ponytail spotted me. "OI!" he yelled, jumping up. "Come here, Taliban!"

His mates jumped up too, and they ran towards us.

"Shit!" yelled Tyler. "Come on, let's move!"

We ran up some stone steps to the main road to get away. It was extra busy, but then it always was.

"Get across the road!" shouted Yusuf.

Tyler and Jem darted through the traffic. Jem was crying, but Tyler grabbed her hand and kept moving.

"Meet back at the cinema!" he shouted at me.

"YEAH!" I replied. I was on the other side of the road, and there was too much traffic. I began to sprint.

Suddenly, I heard Yusuf cry out in pain. I stopped and turned. The men had caught him and were throwing punches and kicks. I hurried back to my friend.

"OI!" I screamed. "LEAVE HIM ALONE!"

I grabbed Yusuf and took a punch to the face. One of them kicked me in the leg, and the pain stopped me short. But I couldn't stand still. I had to move and take Yusuf with me.

"COME ON!" I shouted.

Yusuf's nose was bleeding, and he was crying. He swore at the men, and we set off again. My heartbeat thudded as loudly as their heavy boots on the pavement behind us.

"Cross the road!" Yusuf panted. "We gotta cross the road!"

He squeezed between two cars and got to the middle. But I was too late. The gap in the traffic closed, and I was on my own again. I kept going, praying for another gap in the traffic so that I could cross the road too, but that didn't happen. All the cars and drivers must have seen I was in trouble, but not one of them got out to help me. They just sat and watched.

I felt someone kick me. I fell, and my head banged on the pavement. But I got up and ran on. The men were laughing and shouting, like they were animals chasing prey. They were right behind me, so I had to think fast.

I saw more steps from the road down to the river, and I knew that I had to drop down to the river again. I was fast, but I had to slow the men down. I had to stop running in a straight line. If not, they'd catch me.

I took the steps in two jumps and was back on the wet riverside path. I was very

scared now, but I stayed focused on getting away. I looked straight ahead as I ran, until I got to the next set of stone steps up to the road again. I ran up them. The men were beginning to get tired. I turned my head and saw that one of them was gasping for breath, but Ponytail was still after me.

"SHIT!"

I took the next set of stone steps back to the riverside and did the same thing again. Up and down, up and down, until I was sure I'd get away.

Soon, it was just me running along the riverside, my heart pounding and my lungs burning. But I kept on until I got to the retail park. Only then did I stop. Ponytail and his mates were gone. I was alone and gasping for air, but safe. I stopped to catch my breath and reached for my phone. It wasn't there.

"NO!" I yelled.

I must have dropped it trying to escape. How was I going to call my friends to see where they were? Or my parents? Or the police?

Tyler had said to meet back at the cinema. I pulled my hood over my turban and began to make my way through the retail park.

A sudden screech of brakes and bright headlights made me shiver in fright. It was a battered old Volvo estate.

"You ain't getting away that easy!" I heard Mr Ponytail shout.

He had come after me. I turned back to the river and began to run again. But now my leg hurt from where they'd kicked me, and I was too slow. Someone kicked me over, and this time I hit the ground hard. Another kick got my turban, but it didn't hurt too badly. Then another.

Then I saw Mr Ponytail staring down at me. "I told you to stay away from white girls," he said. "Dirty Taliban prick!"

He spat at me, and then I saw his giant black boot. It was the last thing I saw ...

AFTER

I should have enjoyed that night. I should have

walked Jem home, maybe kissed her goodnight.

Hung around the chicken shop with Yusuf and

Tyler – grabbed some hot wings and a drink.

Found my mum waiting up for me, like she

always did. My dad fast asleep on the sofa,

still wearing his boots, snoring like a hog.

I *should* have been safe to walk down the riverside no matter who I was with, or who I was. But all of that was taken from me. And I can't understand why. Was it my turban? Just my turban? A crown to me, yeah, but just a piece of cloth to those men. To take me away from my life for a piece of cloth they didn't even understand? How do I make sense of that?

It's cold down here. The darkness is all around me, wet and slimy, and without hope. All the things I was, they're all gone. All the things I was gonna be, they are gone too. I am lost in this murky and dirty water, nothing but tears and grief for all the people I once knew and loved.

I was looking forward. I should have been looking back. I should have been watching out for that sudden storm. The one that blew out every candle flame I'd ever lit. Now, there's just silence except for these thoughts.

Just darkness where my light once shone ...

Author Note

A Sudden Storm was inspired by the tragic story of Ricky Reel, a young man from Greater London who disappeared in October 1997, aged twenty. He and his friends were racially abused and attacked in Kingston upon Thames before Ricky vanished. His body was discovered a week later in the River Thames. At first, Ricky's death was ruled accidental. His family refused to accept this though, and they fought to have an inquest, with a jury. In 1999, the jury returned an open verdict, but Ricky's family remain certain that he was the victim of racist killers.

Ricky's Sikh family background and my own were very similar, and his disappearance and tragic death resonated deeply with me. But

A *Sudden Storm* is not Ricky's story. Rather, the tragedy of his murder, and those of so many others, inspired the plot. It is a fictional tale, with fictional characters. My idea is to encourage readers to think about the themes within the book and to ask questions about where prejudice comes from. Where does such hatred lead, and what are the consequences for those who fall victim, their friends and their families?

Ricky's mother, Sukhdev Reel, continues to fight for justice for her son. She has dedicated her life since his death to that goal. Her courage and determination showcase some of the very best human traits, especially when born out of such cruel circumstances.

In 2023, the Metropolitan Police agreed to re-examine Ricky's case. This may be welcome news, but it is two decades too late. If you would like to know more about Sukhdev's fight, and about the real Ricky Reel, please read her book, *Ricky Reel: Silence Is Not An Option*.

Our books are tested
for children and young people by
children and young people.

Thanks to everyone who consulted on
a manuscript for their time and effort in
helping us to make our books better
for our readers.